New Albany and Griffin
street school.

TOUGH ENOUGH
and SASSY

*by Ruth and
Latrobe Carroll*

NEW YORK
HENRY Z. WALCK, INC.   1958

To
William Douglas Morris
Robert Emory Adamson III
George Ross Morris
Ellen McClure Adamson

And, again, we want to thank Tom Alexander, of the Cataloochee Ranch, and Burt Teague, of Asheville, N. C., for their friendly help.

BEANIE Tatum prodded his pony with his heels. "Get along now, Sass," he said. "You and Tough Enough and me, we're goin' to the big ole full-o'-holes tree."

Beanie's little dog, Tough Enough, was barking and running along beside the pony.

Beanie said to Tough Enough and Sassy, "Sure hope we'll see Sweetie Pie and Midnight and Fat Stuff. We're all eatin' so skimpy, maybe those three critters lit out to hunt up somethin' to eat somewheres else. I'm afeared I'll never get to see 'em again."

Sweetie Pie was Beanie's pet skunk, Midnight was his pet talking crow and Fat Stuff was his pet raccoon. Beanie had let them go free on the Great Smoky Mountains farm where he lived with his mother and his father and his brothers and his sisters. He knew they were happier, free. They often took shelter in a gnarled old yellow birch—Beanie called it the full-o'-holes tree—on a mountain slope above the Tatum cabin. They would wait there for Beanie to come and feed them and pet them. They never went near the cabin because they didn't like the big Tatum dogs, old Sour Bone and Nip and Whizz.

Beanie and Sassy and Tough Enough went around a big boulder. And there, just ahead, stood the old tree. It had sheltered wilderness creatures for many, many years. Insects had tormented it, storms had battered it. But now, in the hopefulness of spring, it had put out new golden tassels and tender little leaves.

Tough Enough sniffed at a dark hole in the tree, not far above the ground. He yipped and he wagged his tail.

Chut-chutter-chut, chut-chutter-chut—soft answering sounds were coming from a small black mouth in a little dark, striped face poking out of the opening in the tree. The face was part of Sweetie Pie, Beanie's pet skunk.

Tough Enough put his nose close to Sweetie Pie's nose. He made a small eager noise in his throat. He looked up at another animal lying on a high broad branch. It was gazing down out of eyes with black patches around them.

"Hey, Fat Stuff!" Beanie called up to it. Fat Stuff, Beanie's raccoon, had been snoozing in the sun.

"I don't see Midnight anywheres," Beanie said. "Wonder where in the world that big ole crow can be."

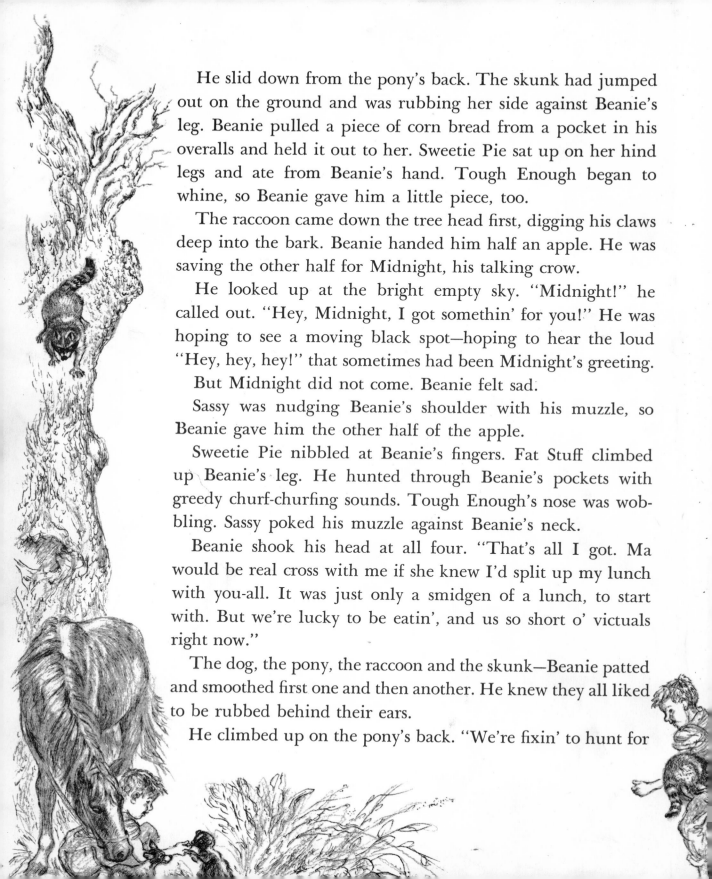

He slid down from the pony's back. The skunk had jumped out on the ground and was rubbing her side against Beanie's leg. Beanie pulled a piece of corn bread from a pocket in his overalls and held it out to her. Sweetie Pie sat up on her hind legs and ate from Beanie's hand. Tough Enough began to whine, so Beanie gave him a little piece, too.

The raccoon came down the tree head first, digging his claws deep into the bark. Beanie handed him half an apple. He was saving the other half for Midnight, his talking crow.

He looked up at the bright empty sky. "Midnight!" he called out. "Hey, Midnight, I got somethin' for you!" He was hoping to see a moving black spot—hoping to hear the loud "Hey, hey, hey!" that sometimes had been Midnight's greeting.

But Midnight did not come. Beanie felt sad.

Sassy was nudging Beanie's shoulder with his muzzle, so Beanie gave him the other half of the apple.

Sweetie Pie nibbled at Beanie's fingers. Fat Stuff climbed up Beanie's leg. He hunted through Beanie's pockets with greedy churf-churfing sounds. Tough Enough's nose was wobbling. Sassy poked his muzzle against Beanie's neck.

Beanie shook his head at all four. "That's all I got. Ma would be real cross with me if she knew I'd split up my lunch with you-all. It was just only a smidgen of a lunch, to start with. But we're lucky to be eatin', and us so short o' victuals right now."

The dog, the pony, the raccoon and the skunk—Beanie patted and smoothed first one and then another. He knew they all liked to be rubbed behind their ears.

He climbed up on the pony's back. "We're fixin' to hunt for

some twisty ole wood," he said to Tough Enough and Sassy, "to pretty up and set plants in and maybe sell in a store down in the valley. If we can only just make some money, maybe we won't all be eatin' so stingy."

He pulled on a rein and turned the pony around, heading him down toward an old jeep road below the Tatum cabin.

Ahead of Beanie his brothers and sisters were walking down the road. Tough Enough caught up with them first, then Sassy and Beanie.

The road twisted and turned, winding through masses of pink laurel blossoms and the soft orange blaze of flame azaleas. The air was vibrant with the humming of honey bees.

Now it was Annie Mae's turn to ride Sassy. Beanie was the youngest and the smallest, so he always got the first and longest

ride. After Annie Mae, it was Irby's turn. Serena got the shortest ride of all. Buck, the oldest and the biggest, was too heavy for the pony. Sassy was only a little more than two years old.

Down, down, down they all went. A lizard whipped itself around and darted away from Tough Enough. A sprinkling of swallowtail butterflies, at the edge of a puddle in the road, flew up in a brilliant cloud and hovered and settled again.

A clearing ahead was flooded with sunshine. Stumps of trees and shrubs had been torn up out of the ground. Here the young Tatums were hoping to find the pieces of wood they wanted. They scattered and began to search.

Sassy was nosing for tender grass and tempting plants.

Tough Enough bounded forward, chasing a grasshopper. It jumped up on a greenbrier vine, safely out of reach. The dog spun around. He nosed out a chipmunk. Yapping, he drove it into its hole. He dug a while at the hole and whined a little. He sniffed at a spider sitting on its web and sneezed when some strands of the web got into his nose.

Beanie looked at him. He smiled. "That little ole Tough Enough," he said, "he never *was* a set-still dog. He sure must have fleas in his feet."

Beanie and his brothers and his sisters were putting gnarled branches and small clusters of roots into four sacks that Buck had brought and tied onto Sassy, two on each side. Part of an old quilt under the sacks kept them from scratching the pony.

Now the sun was low behind the trees on the edge of the clearing. Lofty hemlocks and buckeyes were putting long cool fingers of shade across the open space.

"Let's us quit," said Buck. "We got a right smart load in our tow sacks, and it's gettin' kind o' late."

So they all climbed the steep road back to the cabin. Beanie

led the pony to the back porch. Buck and Irby unloaded him
and put the wood near the back door. Then Beanie rode the
pony to the barn and rubbed him down and put him in his stall.

After supper, Ma picked out the pieces of wood she liked
best—the twisty knotted ones, rich brown or gray or bleached
almost white by the sun. Beanie piled the rest by the fireplace
for kindling wood.

Pa Tatum looked hard at the roots and branches that Ma had saved. He shook his head at her. "I don't rightly know as I hold with this notion o' yourn. How many folks is a-goin' to buy such foolishments? And it all looks like a heap o' work to me."

Ma didn't say a thing. She put a poker into the live coals in the fireplace. When it was red hot she began to burn holes in each piece of wood. With Pa's penknife, she started to dig out the charred places. Beanie and Irby and Buck helped her.

Ma and the boys worked on the wood every evening after the farm chores were done. They made holes big enough to hold small containers. They sandpapered the plant holders until they were smooth and shining as satin.

Annie Mae and Serena went into the forest above the cabin. They dug up partridgeberry and columbine and galax—they

called it coltsfoot—with plenty of rich earth around the roots. They put the plants into little tin cans. Ma had cut some cans in half with Pa's tin-shears. She had scalloped the edges and bent them down and under just a little, so they wouldn't cut anybody.

After she had set the cans, with the plants in them, into the wooden holders, all the Tatums stood off and looked at the woods pretties. That was what they called them. They were smiling—all but Pa.

"I declare," said Ma, "they're the prettiest things in the cove!"

"Might could be," said Pa. "But who'd be tetched in the head enough to pay good hard money for an ole piece o' wood and an ole weed and half an ole tin can?"

The next day all the Tatums went down the mountain in the Tatum truck. All the pretties went, too. The truck stopped at a store where a woman named Mrs. Gudger sold things the mountain people had made.

Mrs. Gudger peered at the pretties through the thick lenses of her glasses. She lifted her eyebrows as high as she could make them go.

"I don't know for certain sure if folks will buy 'em," she said. "Ain't many tourists round now. But I'll try hard to sell 'em. They're real nice." She looked down at Beanie. "But I know what *I* want to buy, young man. Your pretty pony."

Beanie's eyes widened. His mouth opened a little.

"If ever you want your Pa to sell him," Mrs. Gudger went on, "I'll give a right smart sum for him. My little daughter, my Sally, she's seen you ridin' him. She's hankerin' after him or one just like him."

Beanie stared at her. He couldn't say a word. It was Pa who spoke. He said, "Thank you kindly for your offer, ma'am."

The Tatums said good-by and left the store. Outside, as they were walking toward their truck, Beanie said, "Sell Sass? Mrs. Gudger's an ole ganderhead."

Ma shook her head at him. "Beanie Tatum!" she said.

"Looks like Mrs. Gudger ain't overly smart," Buck said carefully, with a sideways glance at Ma.

"Why does she think we'd sell the pony?" asked Annie Mae.

"Reckon she's a mite addlepated," said Irby.

"We'll never sell Sass," said Serena. "Never."

Pa didn't say a thing. Beanie studied his face, hoping to learn what he was thinking. There was a grim look back deep in his eyes. Beanie peered up at his mother's face. The corners of her mouth looked sad.

Did Pa think he needed money so bad that he'd have to sell Sassy? Beanie was sure Pa wouldn't do a thing like that. Not now. But would times get so hard that Pa would just have to? Beanie wondered and worried.

Soon the Tatums were on their way back to their farm. Beside Pa on the front seat were Ma and Serena and Annie Mae. Beanie and Irby and Buck were in the back, sitting on the floor of the truck.

Buck said, "We just got to make money, a whole slew o' money. Enough so Pa can pay off what he owes at the general store for seed and gasoline and food. It'll take squeezin' and schemin' to make any payment a-tall this year. That pesky dry spell last year shriveled up our tobacco and corn and cabbages and such and liked to a-ruined us."

Irby said, "If we can sell some woods pretties, maybe we'll make do some sort o' how."

"But s'posin' we just can't make anything that sells?" asked Buck. "Then what'll we do? These is pinchin' times. How'll we keep on eatin'?"

Beanie said, "And what about Tough Enough and Sass and Fat Stuff and Sweetie Pie and my kitty, Bobcat Bob, and our ole horse, Pal, and ole Sour Bone and Nip and Whizz and the cats, Barbie and Cookie and Pinky Nose? How about *them*?"

The bottom of Beanie's stomach felt cold and queer. "Sassy," he said. "Mrs. Gudger, she said she'd buy Sassy and give a right smart sum for him. And Pa just said, 'Thank you kindly for your offer, ma'am.' That was all he said."

"Sass is still a small-like horse," said Buck, "too young to do much work on the farm. He's just only made a start at learnin' to pull a plow. Old Pal still does all the real sure-'nough work."

"We could get along all right without Sass," Beanie admitted. "We could do without his totin' that ole wood we make pretties out of. Us young-uns, we'd get tireder, doin' the totin' ourselves and walkin' more'n we do now. But we'd make out all right without Sassy Boy."

A lump came into Beanie's throat. Tears filled his eyes. He winked them away, but more tears came welling.

"Sassy . . ." he said. "I can't give up Sassy. I just . . . can't."

NOW the wild strawberries were ripening in the valley. So all the Tatum children and Tough Enough and Sassy started off for an apple orchard where strawberries grew thick beneath the trees. Buck's dog, Nip, and Irby's dog, Whizz, usually went off rabbit hunting together. But this time they came along, too.

They all reached the bank of a creek, a stream with a swinging bridge stretching across. Beanie's brothers and sisters hurried to the bridge and out onto it. They were running and skipping and jumping.

"Goll*eee*!" yelled Irby.

"Great day!" cried Serena.

Something was happening under their feet. The bridge was moving. It was weaving up and down. It was flowing with a motion like an ocean wave.

Serena and Buck and Irby and Annie Mae held onto the long rope railings at the sides of the bridge. They were shouting and laughing.

Tough Enough and Nip and Whizz had started across, too. But as soon as they felt the bridge lurch they turned and rushed back to shore, whining and yapping and yelping. They wouldn't go across until the young Tatums got tired and the bridge was hanging still.

Sassy was too heavy for the bridge. Beanie had ridden him into the creek at a shallow place.

All of a sudden Sassy turned and headed downstream. Beanie
pulled on a rein, trying to bring his head around. But Sassy
kept splashing on down the creek.·

Beanie grinned. "I'd almost gone and forgot what a swimmin'
little ole horse you are," he said to Sassy. "So now you're
headin' for deep water. Lan's alive!"

Beanie's brothers and sisters were running along the bank.
They were shouting and shouting at Sassy. Tough Enough and
Nip and Whizz were chasing after them. All three dogs were
barking.

Tough Enough plunged into the stream. He swam out to
Sassy and got hold of his tail. He tried to pull him back, but he

couldn't. He got water down his throat and glugged and
coughed and let go. Whining, he headed back toward shore.

"I'll fetch Sass if I can," said Buck. He waded out to the
pony and got hold of the reins. He turned the little horse toward
the bank. Soon Sassy was climbing up out of the creek.

"Stubborn," Buck panted, "like a mule. Plumb bawkified.
He come out just only 'cause he was good and ready, I reckon."

They all started off again. At last they reached the orchard.
The scent of strawberries in the sun was rich in Beanie's nostrils.
"Smells lickin' good," he said. And he popped a fat red berry
into his mouth.

At first the young Tatums were eating more berries than
they were putting into their pails. Beanie thought he had never
tasted such delicious little things. Each ripe berry had stored

up the best of the spring and the best of the early summer. Each was full of freshness, full of wild sweetness.

Serena spoke firmly. "Hey, you-all, looka here! We'd better stop eatin' so many berries. I don't aim to eat another one"—she looked at her brothers and sister—"and nobody else had better, either."

Buck nodded. "Serena's right, and that's a fact. Wouldn't be right, nohow. Remember, we got to give half of all we pick to the folks that own this orchard."

Annie Mae said, "If we keep eatin' 'em, Ma and Serena and

I won't have enough to make jars and jars and jars of strawberry jam."

"And we won't have jam to leave with Mrs. Gudger, to sell," said Beanie. He looked at Sassy tethered to an apple tree. "I sure am hungry a lot o' the time. But we don't want Sally Gudger to get Sass."

So the young Tatums really went to work, picking the berries and hulling them before they dropped them into their pails.

On their way home they all went swimming in a clear pond just below an abandoned mill. Long after the children and the

dogs had had enough swimming, Sassy kept going around in wide circles in the millpond. The young Tatums and the dogs were sitting on the bank, ready to start home.

Buck laughed. He said, "Always waitin' on that horse."

At last the pony came stepping and sloshing out of the pool. Every time he put a foot down it made a quick little puddle. Tough Enough went racing round and round him, making a great yapping fuss.

Back in the barn, Beanie brushed and curried Sassy until his new summer coat was smooth and glossy.

Now the Tatum farm was a very busy place. The cows, the pigs, the chickens, Sassy and old Pal, the four dogs, the four cats—looking after them all was only part of the work the Tatums had to do. There was also the labor of the crops.

Pa Tatum was trying to teach Sassy how to pull a plow. It wasn't easy for either Pa or Sass.

Sometimes the pony would stop pulling. His mouth would reach out for tender leaves or reach down for young grass. Even when Pa slapped him with the reins and yelled "Come-*up*, come-*up*!" he wouldn't move an inch. He would just stand and chew.

Beanie would pull on the reins and shout, "Hey, Tough, go get Sass, make him go!" The little dog would come hurrying and yapping. He would nip Sassy's heels. Sassy would strain forward again.

"He's just plumb contrary," Pa would sometimes say, as the plowshare bit in once more. "But that Tough, he knows a trick or two."

Sassy learned slowly. Beanie used to walk very near him, holding on to the bridle rein close to the bit, leading him as he pulled.

Beanie liked to listen to small tearing sounds as the steel blade cut little roots. He liked to watch the earth curl back in a red-brown wave. He loved the earthy smell.

After a soft steady rain, Beanie and his brothers and sisters helped Pa set out tobacco seedlings in the plowed field that was moist and waiting. With hickory pegs, they made holes to put the seedlings in. They chopped out weeds in the vegetable garden, in the cabbage patch and the cornfield.

Once, working in the field of corn, Beanie said to Buck, "I sure do miss Midnight. But if that ole crow ever comes flappin' back he'll steal a heap o' this corn, and that's a true fact."

No more rain came down as the days passed and passed. Every evening before bedtime Pa would look up at the sky sparkling with stars. Every morning he would watch a cloudless dawn come up, and his face would set in deep sad lines.

One shimmering day, Ma Tatum said to the children, "Might could be our crops'll fail us again. I've been a-studyin' more ways o' makin' money. You young-uns go git me a mess o' little bitty acorns and hemlock cones, and I'll show you a thing or two."

Off went Beanie and Irby and Annie Mae and Buck and Serena and Sassy and Tough Enough, off to a hemlock forest. Warm arrows of light, shooting down through the dark green branches, reddened the little cones and needles scattered over the forest floor. The air was full of a faint, dry fragrance.

Sassy had a load of baskets fastened onto his back. The young Tatums filled them with hemlock cones.

Another day they started off toward an oak forest. They took

a roundabout trail that led them first to their favorite place. They called it the water slide. There, a mountain stream had flowed over slabs of rock for countless years, making them smooth and slippery. The stream ran sweeping and frothing into a deep pool below.

One by one, the young Tatums sat down at the top of the slide. One by one, they pushed themselves through shallow water, deeper and deeper in, until the current caught them.

When Beanie's turn came he sucked in an excited breath. The water carried him down over the slippery surface, faster and faster and faster. It landed him, ker-*plop,* in the pool.

He gasped. He squealed. He gulped in a mouthful of water and blew it out in a spray. He dived down into deep cold wetness and made a curving turn. Up he came, up, up, up till his head popped out and the sun was shining on his face.

"Whee-e-e-ew!" he shouted. He shook his head and laughed. "It's a heap o' fun!"

Tough Enough didn't like the slide. He stayed on the bank and barked at everybody. But Sassy swam round and round in the deep pool. The children had to look sharp, not to land on top of him.

Beanie said, "I reckon we'd all like to lallygag round here and pleasure ourselves all day, but slidin' and swimmin' don't gather any acorns."

The young Tatums and the dog and the pony went on their way again. At last they reached the oak forest. High winds had knocked acorns down onto the ground. The acorns were tiny, like little buttons—just beginning to poke out of their acorn-cups. The children picked up as many as they could find.

Then Beanie and Buck and Irby climbed the trees with the lowest branches. They pulled off all the acorns they could reach. They tossed them down to Annie Mae and Serena, to put into the baskets.

Whenever a branch was too high, Sass would help Beanie climb a tree. Irby would hold the pony still while Beanie got up on the pony's back. Then Beanie could reach the branch.

Sassy found lush grass to eat. When going-home time came he wouldn't go. Beanie watched him cropping tender blades. "No wonder Sass wants to stick around here," he said. "You can't handily blame him. He's got good juicy pickin's."

Beanie thought of the dry parched grass in the Tatum pastures, of the hard red-clay soil that showed through in places, of the crops thirsty for moisture.

He and his brothers and sisters let Sassy graze a while. But at last they could wait no longer. Beanie pulled on the pony's reins. Irby and Annie Mae and Buck and Serena pushed and shoved him. But he spread his legs just like a mule. He would not budge.

Beanie said to Tough Enough, "Hey, Tough, make him go!" The dog began to nip Sassy's heels. He gave a lot of "git-along-Sassy" barks. He made the pony follow the children.

On the way home, Tough Enough left the trail. He darted off into the woods on a small side trip of his own. The young Tatums saw a chance to tease him a little.

Not far ahead of them was a strange tree. Heavy rains had washed the soil away from its roots and had hollowed out a dark cave under its trunk. Now it looked as if it were standing on tiptoe.

Beanie tethered Sass to the rough brown column of a root. He and his brothers and sisters crawled under the tree. They hid in the dimness. Nobody spoke. Everybody waited. Everybody listened. Everybody looked.

They heard a faraway "Yipe!" It sounded like a puzzled

question, Beanie thought. Then came an impatient "Yipe-yipe-yipe." Annie Mae began a little giggle, but she pressed her hand against her mouth and smothered it.

The little dog came bounding through the forest, not straight but in a zigzag way. It was plain from his uncertain running that he couldn't see the young Tatums anywhere. Every now and then he gave a shrill, worried yip. But when he got back to the trail he put his sniffing nose to the ground. It led him to the cave under the tree.

He scurried in, barking fast and high. He chased the children round and round the great roots. He jumped and he jumped up on them, licking and licking their hands. He did his best to leap high enough so he could lick their faces.

"Lan's alive!" said Beanie. "That little ole Tough Enough, he's plumb bustin' out o' himself."

When the boys and girls got back to the cabin, Ma had a big darning needle all ready, and some stout dark-brown thread. She showed Serena and Annie Mae how to make necklaces out of the acorns and the hemlock cones. Whenever it was hard to push the needle through the toughest acorn-cups, Buck did it for them. He and Irby and Beanie gave each necklace a coat of white shellac, to preserve it.

As the children worked they often sang old mountain ballads —songs they had heard their parents and grandparents sing, time and time again. Beanie knew why he and the others were singing so much. It was to cover up their worry over the long dry spell. Would this year's drought be as bad as last year's? Would all the crops die under the bright hot sun?

The Tatums took the necklaces down to Mrs. Gudger the next day. When she saw them her eyebrows went up toward her

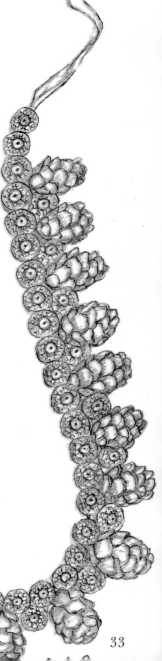

hair. "Well, I *never!*" she said. "What-all you folks won't think of, next. You're master hands for notions. They're real nice— mighty nice."

The Tatums smiled at her. She looked at Beanie. "My Sally pesters me 'most all the time," she said, "to buy her that pony o' yours."

The Tatums stopped smiling. They didn't smile all the way home.

When the truck stopped near the cabin, Beanie and Tough Enough were the first ones out. Beanie ran to the barn with the little dog close behind him. He threw his arms around the pony's neck. He hugged him hard, as if to keep anyone from taking him away.

He looked down at Tough Enough. "If we get poorer and poorer," he said to the dog, "maybe Pa will just *have* to sell Sass. Sweetie Pie and Fat Stuff will maybe go where they can get more to eat, just like Midnight did. Maybe . . . maybe the only pets I'll have left will be my kitty, Bobcat Bob . . . and you."

ONE day, Pa came driving back from a trip down to the valley to sell baskets of blackberries the children had picked. Beanie watched him come. Pa was driving the truck unusually fast. He stopped it with a jerk. Its tires churned the dirt. Little stones flew up behind and rattled against the fenders.

Pa blew the horn gaily three times. He came striding toward the cabin. He had many ways of walking; Beanie knew them all. Now Pa was stepping right along in his can't-wait-to-git-home way.

Beanie went running to meet him. Pa caught him by both hands and lifted him off his feet and began to swing him round and round. In front of Beanie's eyes everything went swirling.

Ma and Serena and Buck and Irby and Annie Mae had run out. They stood looking and laughing.

While Pa was spinning like a tall slow top he was shouting out words: "Got news . . . for you-all—good news. I was talkin' . . . to Mrs. Gudger . . . a while ago and . . . *guess what*. She sold three o' your woods pretties."

Pa stopped whirling. Beanie's feet fumbled for the ground and found it. For a moment it was hard for him to stand, he was so happily dizzy.

Pa said, "Mrs. Gudger sold a necklace, and she sold the plant-holder Beanie said looked like an ole dragon. And that twisty ole laurel root with the coltsfoot a-growin' in it—that sold, too."

Beanie gave an excited jump. Now all the Tatums were talking at once. Nobody could understand anybody, so they all stopped. That gave Pa a chance to go on: "Mrs. Gudger said for us to make some more pretties for her to try and sell—and some more, too, for a store in Waynesville. There's more comers and goers likely to buy 'em in Waynesville, more folks touristin' round."

And so, after supper, the Tatums began to make more woods pretties. This time Pa was helping.

All of a sudden a cool puff of air pushed at the window curtains. They billowed out. Pa stopped working on a piece of wood. He went striding to the window. He looked out at the sky.

Beanie heard a sound. The others heard it, too. It was a gentle pattering on the split-oak shingles of the cabin's roof.

"Rain!" cried Beanie. "It's come on to rain."

"Rain! Rain! Rain!" yelled Buck.

Beanie ran out of the cabin, beyond a sheltering oak tree. He lifted up his face so he could feel the cool drops on it. With every breath he drew he could smell the good smell of the rain.

He went hurrying straight to the tobacco field. He squatted

down among the plants and looked and looked at them. They were wet and gleaming—drinking gratefully, he thought, in tiny sucks and sips. He put out his hand and touched a leaf. It felt cool and firm and full.

He heard a yipping and yowping and yapping. A wet Tough Enough came running. He hurled himself on Beanie. Beanie was so very wet, the dog couldn't make him any wetter.

Back at the cabin, a little later, he found Pa and Ma on the porch. Pa's eyes were searching the sky as if to measure the moisture it still held. At last Pa said, "Reckon we're a-goin' to have us a right smart bit o' rain." He smiled his biggest smile.

Ma closed her eyes for a moment. "The Lord be praised," she said.

All the next day it rained and rained and rained. Working in the cabin, Beanie could hear soft drummings and drippings and tricklings.

Pa said, "I calculate we'll have us some real good crops this year. Only question is, the money price we'll git. I've seen the time when a mighty good crop brought a mighty poor price."

Summer ended. Autumn lay over the land.

The mountains glowed with colors—the rich plum-purple of the dogwoods, the orange and yellow of the sassafras, the gold of the tulip trees and the hickories, the steady flames of the maples, the crimson of the black-gum leaves that waved like little flags.

Now it was hickory-nut time. Early one Saturday morning the young Tatums were leaving the barn on their way to gather nuts. They were taking Tough Enough and Sassy.

All of a sudden, Beanie heard a hoarse distant call: *"Hey, hey, hey!"*

"It's Midnight!" he shouted. "Midnight's come back. Let's us go to the ole full-o'-holes tree. Maybe he's roostin' on it."

They all hurried to the tree, but they didn't see Midnight there, or hear that hoarse call again.

"Reckon it was some other ole crow," said Buck.

So they all went on their way toward a stand of hickory trees on a lonesome mountain. A small sharp breeze was blowing, bringing a scent Beanie loved—the moldy smell of dead leaves on the ground. He drew deep stinging breaths. "It's whizzin' cold," he said. "The air's got little teeth in it."

The breeze grew stronger, pushing against the trees. Hundreds of leaves, thousands of leaves were falling. They filled the air, fluttering down and blowing over the ground. Just as far as Beanie could see, the forest floor was tumbling and shimmering and dancing.

Sometimes a gust, sweeping along, would make a rustling river, a torrent of reds and golds.

Serena was riding Sassy. The cutting wind made the pony gallop; it got into Tough Enough's blood. Sometimes the little dog went running along beside Sassy. Every now and then he went rushing away among the flying leaves, almost hidden by the brilliant shifting smother.

The young Tatums and the dog and the pony went down from a high ridge into a hollow where leaves had piled up deep. Here, grape vines had climbed locust trees. Some of their long tough stems were looping down.

"Grapevine swings!" cried Beanie.

He caught hold of a vine stem. He backed away till it pulled

taut, and then he ran forward to get up speed. The long rope of the vine stem took him off his feet and up and out into the air. At the very end of his outward swing he let go, over heaped-up leaves. Falling was fine, and landing, *plop,* was even better. It was like coming down hard on a heap of soft thick pillows.

Beanie's brothers and sisters were swinging and falling and plopping, too.

At last Beanie said, "Swingin' and prankin' don't gather any hickory nuts to sell."

So they all went on up to the hickory trees and settled down to the steady work of filling their baskets.

Beanie didn't tether Sass to one of the trees. Nearby, the grass grew thick and green. So Beanie let the pony graze free.

Tough Enough was exploring in a sniffing way. All of a sudden his big ears went up; his nose began to wobble.

Sassy blew air through his nostrils. The sudden sound made Beanie look at him. The pony had cleared his nose. He had lifted his head high and was turning and turning it. He seemed to be testing the air in all directions.

Beanie said to his brothers and sisters, "I've never seen Sass act thataway. Looks like his nose is bringin' him news."

The next quick noise came from Tough Enough. He gave a questioning yip. He ran to a nearby thicket and plunged in.

"Reckon Tough's after a squirrel," said Beanie. He looked at the green tangle where the dog had disappeared. He listened. For a moment he could not hear a thing. Then Tough Enough began a frantic barking. Other sounds, too, were coming out of the thicket—snortings and heavy stampings.

Buck called out, "If that there's a squirrel, it's a powerful big one."

Sassy gave a shrill snort. He wheeled. He burst through a wall of bushes, then plunged down the mountain slope.

A moment later Tough Enough came rushing out. Behind him charged a huge wild boar. On the creature's back and neck his dark-gray hackles were bristling. His little eyes were red with rage. His sharp tusks gleamed white in the sun.

The young Tatums stood rigid, watching.

The little dog dodged the boar's first rush, then turned and tried to bite his ear. That took him within reach of the creature's tusks, now lowered almost to the ground. The beast brought his head up in a sudden thrust. He was trying to slit the dog open.

His tusks slashed nothing but empty air. Tough Enough had leaped away. The great beast swung around; he was quick

in spite of his size. He was breathing hard. Strings of froth hung from his jaws.

Beanie was shaking with fear—fear that his little dog did not have long to live. He saw a big stone and picked it up.

"Don't fling that rock!" Buck yelled. "That boar's crosser'n a hornet. He'd maybe kill you dead. Run! Everybody run!"

The young Tatums turned; they ran as fast as they could

toward the trail back home. Beanie could hear his dog's voice lifted in terror. The shrill yiping grew fainter. Fainter. The sounds of the children running along the trail, the sounds of their panting breaths—those were the only noises in the forest now.

The boys and girls stopped running. Buck put his arm around Beanie. When he had caught his breath he said, "Don't you go frettin'. That feisty little feller, he bit off more'n he could chew, but I figger he got clean away. He could scrouge right into a holler log or into a ground-hog hole."

"Tough, he'll pick a fight," said Irby, "but when he sees it's plumb foolish he'll light out after a while."

"We'll find him settin' on the front porch when we get home," Serena said gently, "actin' like he never started nothin' a-tall."

Annie Mae said, "And Sass will be there, too, down by the barn—you'll see."

Beanie drew a quivering breath. He said, "Tough, he was tryin' to keep that boar from hurtin' us bad, Tough was."

Serena nodded. Her eyes looked large and soft. "He was tryin' to protect us," she said. "Now he's waitin' for us, I reckon."

But when the young Tatums got home they didn't see Tough Enough. Beanie called and called and whistled and whistled. Tough Enough didn't come. Neither did Sass. The young Tatums looked everywhere on the farm. They could not find the pony or the dog.

That evening after supper the other dogs—Sour Bone and Nip and Whizz—were fed. And so were the cats—Cookie and Barby and Pinky Nose and Bobcat Bob.

But no little big-eared dog came to get his supper.

Beanie went out to the barn again and again, but Sass wasn't there. He felt sick at heart.

"Pa, let's us go look for Tough Enough and Sass," Beanie begged. "Can't we go right now, Pa?"

"Please, Pa," said Annie Mae.

"Oh, Pa!" said Serena.

Buck and Irby pressed close to Pa, waiting for his answer.

Pa shook his head. "Can't do nothin' till afore sunup. We got to go a far piece to hunt for that pony and that dog. No use knockin' round in the dark. Good daylight's the time."

Pa looked at the young Tatums. His eyes were kind. "Don't you-all go gittin' down in the mouth," he said.

Beanie tried to speak, but his words turned into a gulp.

"It does beat all," Pa went on. "That big hunk o' hog, he musta been a-traipsin', a-roamin' far away on his own. It's a seldom thing you'll hear tell o' any wild boars nearer'n a hundred miles from here. They mostly stick close to the Nantahala Forest in the lonesomest part o' the thickety woods. It sure is the beatin'est thing."

That night Beanie couldn't sleep. His wide-open eyes kept seeing pictures in the dark—frightening pictures of Tough Enough and the boar.

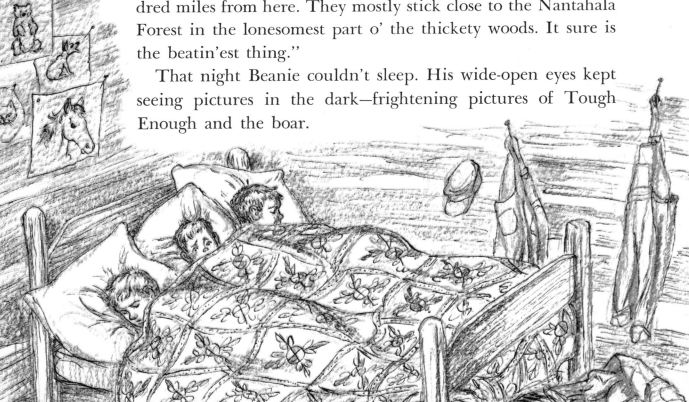

PA was up long before dawn, oiling his gun. Ma put up a snack for him and Buck and Irby and Beanie. The four left the cabin while it was still quite dark outside.

Pa's dog, old Sour Bone, didn't go along. He was too old for hunting. He took the cows to pasture every morning and brought them home in the evening.

Nip and Whizz went with Pa and the boys. Nip had a chain attached to his collar and so did Whizz. Buck and Irby were holding on to the chains. They didn't want the dogs to go chasing after the boar.

Pa and the boys and the dogs had to cross a lofty ridge. Up on the top they found themselves in cold thin fog with glints of sun striking through. The mist had frozen in a layer of rime ice. Every leaf still on the trees, every pine needle, every blade of withered grass, even every weed was a delicate thing of purest white. Ice blossoms, ice feathers, ice ferns were shining all around, but Beanie hardly noticed them; he was so worried.

They all crossed the top of the ridge, then they went zig-
zagging down, down, down. They reached the place where Tough
Enough had tried to fight the boar.

The dogs put their noses to the trampled, torn-up ground.
Half wild with excitement, they were pulling this way and that.
It was all Buck and Irby could do to hold on to their chains.

Pa was searching the ground. "No blood trail," he said. "I
figger the boar didn't get to Tough."

Happiness filled Beanie. Warm happiness. It went through
him like a wave.

"If we can find Sass," said Pa, "we'll find Tough Enough,
sure as sunup."

"Sass lit out thataway," said Buck. He was pointing at a mass

of bushes. "He went a-scootin' through down there, remember?"

Buck and Irby had to drag the dogs away to the place where Sassy had plunged in.

Beanie pulled a cloth from a pocket, a cloth he had used for rubbing Sassy down. He held it close to the dogs' noses. Buck talked to Nip and Irby talked to Whizz. Nip was the best trail dog. Before long he understood what his master wanted him to do—go find Sass. He searched and searched the ground with the end of his nose.

He lifted his voice in a deep baying. He went pushing through the bushes, dragging Buck after him.

All the others followed Nip and Buck down the mountain slope. Whizz was barking, making a great to-do.

It was a rough downward scramble for Pa and the boys. On and on they went; and always, from ahead, came Nip's deep bell-like baying.

Beanie called out, "Listen, listen!"

"Can't hear nothin' with all this ruckus," yelled Pa.

Above the baying and barking it came again: a shrill "Yipe, yipe!"

"It's Tough Enough!" Beanie shouted.

The little dog came tearing through underbrush. He hurled himself at Beanie. Beanie caught him and held him tight. Tough Enough licked Beanie's chin and did his best to lick his nose. He was whimpering.

He began to struggle in Beanie's arms. He seemed to be trying to get away, so Beanie put him down on the ground. Tough Enough ran back in the direction he had come from,

then he stopped and turned and barked and barked at Beanie.

"I reckon Tough wants us to come along after him," Beanie called out. "Maybe he'll take us to Sass!"

Buck and Irby unleashed Nip and Whizz. Everybody started to follow Tough Enough. The little dog went scrambling down the mountain.

He stopped. He lifted his head. He howled. Nip and Whizz were running around, sniffing and barking and baying. Above all the hullabaloo Beanie heard a shrill whinny.

"It's *Sass!*" he shouted. He ran toward the sound as fast as he could.

All of a sudden he saw Sassy's head. It was sticking out of the ground, out of a sort of deep trench.

"Oh, Pa!" cried Beanie. "Sass went and fell in a hole. He did. Oh, *Pa!*"

Beanie ran to the edge of the cut in the earth. He knelt near

Sassy's head. He reached out and patted and petted him. Sassy stamped and whinnied. Beanie could feel him trembling.

"Sassy Boy," he asked, "are you bad hurt?"

The pony snorted and tossed his head and pushed against the sides of the cut.

Beanie began to talk to him. His voice was calm and low and gentle. "Don't you fret, Sassy Boy, now don't you fret yourself." Sassy stopped trembling and stood still.

Pa pointed to a pile of shiny mica nearby and then at the cut Sassy was in. He said, "I calculate that hole was a little ole one-man mica mine, a cut somebody made when he was a-diggin' for mica sheets he could sell. It's so choked up with weeds and vines and bushes and all, I reckon Sass didn't see it when he come a-tearin' down the mountain."

Beanie cried, "Pa, what'll we do?"

Pa Tatum put his hand on Beanie's shoulder. "It's right much of a problem," he said. "I'm a-studyin' it. First off, let's us see what kind o' shape Sassy's in, far as we can."

Pa lay down on his stomach at the edge of the cut, just as

close to the pony as he could get. He reached out. He parted a green tangle close to Sassy's side. He peered down.

"Can't tell much about the little feller from up here," he said. "I just can't rightly tell." Pa stopped talking. He stood up. He went on, "I'd climb down in that cut and look Sass over and feel him over good, and we'd know right straight off. But it's too close quarters to be in with a stompin' shovin' horse. It'd be easy to git stomped. So I'm not a-climbin' down in there."

Beanie said quickly, "Let *me*. . ."

Pa broke in, "Nobody's a-climbin' down, you hear? *Nobody*. Now I'll tell you what. Buck and me, we'll go back to the farm. There's an ole loggin' road back down yonder. We'll fetch us an ax and a pickax and a couple o' shovels. Then we'll dig a kind of a slopin' ditch, like, so Sass can walk plumb out o' the hole he's in."

Instead of leaving at once, Pa squatted down near the edge of the mica mine cut. He pulled a brown paper bag from a pocket. "High time for the sandwich snack Ma put up for us," he said.

The four began to eat. Tough Enough sat down very close to Beanie's grape-jelly sandwich. His tongue came out and ran around his mouth. Beanie handed him some scraps.

Sassy began to stamp. He gave a frightened whinny.

Pa said in his kindly voice, "Hey, little feller, just you git a-holt o' yourself. We'll dig you out directly. Just you git a-holt."

When Pa and Buck and Nip and Whizz had gone, Beanie said to Irby, "When a pony falls in a hole he can hurt himself bad, real bad. Irby . . . do you s'pose . . . Sass went and broke a leg?"

Irby frowned. "Well," he said, "Sass is so kind o' restless and fitified, maybe a leg or somethin' is painin' him. But he'd be

fitified anyhow, stuck down in that hole. We just can't tell, not till we get him out."

"Lan's alive!" said Beanie. "I didn't know waitin' and waitin' could be such a frazzlin' thing."

The brothers fell silent. Tough Enough lay down as close to Sassy's muzzle as he could get. He and the pony touched noses.

The only sound in the forest was a bird's repeated call—the *tsip, tsip, tsip* of a junco.

A little white-footed mouse peeked out at Beanie from under a pile of maple leaves. Its eyes were big and bright. Beanie watched it. He didn't move. It came out and sat up. It washed its face with a flutter of its paws.

Tough Enough yawned with a yawny sound. It was very faint, but the mouse whisked back under the leaves.

The pony nickered in a worried way. Beanie patted him. He began to sing. He hoped his voice would comfort Sassy. He was singing an old mountain ballad called "Mole in the Ground."

Irby joined in. Then the brothers swung into "Old Smoky" and "Swannanoa Tunnel."

The sun was standing well above a ridge when Nip and Whizz came scurrying and scuffling from under a tall rhododendron bush. They were barking. Tough Enough was barking back.

Beanie said, "It won't be long afore Pa and Buck turn up here at Sassy's mica mine."

Beanie was right. Soon Pa Tatum and Buck returned, carrying an ax and two shovels and a pickax. Ma and Serena and Annie Mae came with them. They were bringing dinner for everybody—ham and cornbread and apples and a big jar of milk. They had water and oats for Sassy.

Before work began, the Tatums ate their dinner. Then Pa
and Buck started digging. After they got tired, Beanie and Irby
dug. Plainly it would take all afternoon to dig a sloping ditch

down to Sassy. Rocks in the way had to be pried up; bushes and saplings had to be cut down and grubbed out.

At last Pa Tatum and Buck were working quite close to the mica mine cut. They began to dig slowly and carefully. They didn't want to hurt the pony with their sharp tools.

As they started digging down at the edge of the cut, Sassy grew even more restless. He began to snort and stamp, as if he wanted them to hurry up. And Tough Enough was barking and getting in the way of the work, telling them to hurry, too. Beanie had to pull him away.

Slowly the ditch grew deeper. As Pa was spading the earth away from the pony's chest, Sassy kept poking his head into the ditch and struggling to jump out. He was such a nosy nuisance that Irby had to grip the reins tightly, to hold him back.

At last the ditch was down almost to the bottom of the mica mine cut. Pa Tatum tossed his shovel up on the bank. He took hold of the pony's reins, close to the bit.

Beanie and Tough Enough were peering down over the edge, looking hard at the pony.

Beanie caught his breath. "We'll know," he thought to himself. "In a couple o' jiffies we'll know if Sassy Boy hurt himself bad."

The pony stepped up and lurched forward. He was quivering with eagerness to get out of the trap that had held him so long. He came hobbling at an awkward gait, but Pa had to move fast to stay ahead of him.

Up on the bank, Beanie and Tough Enough were running, keeping up with the pony. Beanie could feel his heart pounding. Again and again he was asking himself, "Why is Sassy limpin' so?"

As soon as the pony was out of the ditch, Pa stopped him and handed the reins to Beanie. Beanie pressed his cheek against Sassy's head. He held him while Pa's fingers went over him, feeling for broken bones.

Tough Enough was racing round and round Sassy, yapping shrill yaps. Ma and Serena and Buck and Irby and Annie Mae were petting and smoothing the pony and saying gentle things to him.

Pa's fingers stopped pressing and probing. He gave Sassy a pat. He put up his hand and tilted his hat back on his head. He was grinning.

"Reckon Sass got stiff and kind o' lame," he said, "from standin' boxed in for hours and hours, all chilly and cramped up. But . . . he's sound as a hickory nut."

Beanie gave a whoop and a jump. He had never felt so happy. "Sound as a hickory nut!" he shouted.

Soon Sassy was drinking water out of a pail, making thirsty sucking noises. And then he was eating oats out of a little bag.

"Let's rub his legs," said Beanie, "so they won't be so stiff."

He and his brothers and sisters began to give Sassy's legs a

brisk going over. The pony nuzzled them gently. Once his teeth found a button on the back of Annie Mae's jacket and closed on it and pulled it off. Annie Mae had to open his mouth and get the wet button out.

In spite of all the rubbing, Sassy was still slightly stiff—he still limped just a little—when the Tatums and their dogs started back along the old logging road. But soon the lameness left him.

After they all got home, Ma fixed a hot bran mash for Sassy. Beanie helped her. He carried the steaming mash to the pony. Sassy's nostrils widened, he gave a sniffing snort, then he poked his muzzle down into the pail.

Tough Enough stood close, ears up and tail wagging.

Beanie watched. He listened to munching sounds. His eyes were shining. He patted Sassy. "Stout little ole horse," he said. "Fallin' into that hole didn't do you a mite o' harm—no, not a dab o' harm. It didn't."

That evening Beanie was picking over some pieces of mica he had gathered by the abandoned mine. He held up one sheet and

turned and turned it in the lamp light. He was studying brown and silvery patches. They gleamed richly.

"Lan's alive!" he said. "This here one's got shapes in it. They look kind o' like an ole rooster."

He rummaged around and picked up another piece. "I can see an ole fish in this one," he said.

Now the other Tatums were laughing, but Beanie insisted, "Yes, I can, sure 'nough."

He pulled his penknife out of an overalls pocket. He scratched away at some small thick sheets of mica. He showed them to Ma.

She said, "I declare! There *is* an ole rooster in there. And I can see that ole fish, too."

Beanie peeled off the rough outer layers. With Pa's tin-shears he trimmed the mica where he had scratched lines on it. He said, "We'll maybe have us a mess o' new pretties from Sassy's mica mine to sell."

His brothers and sisters helped peel some pieces until they were quite thin and almost as clear as glass. The yellow lamp light, the red table cloth, the dotted green window curtains—all were reflected in them. Ma took the penknife and etched in some last clever scratches.

They finished up a shiny rooster, a fish, a pig, a duck, a pony, a rabbit and a hoptoad. Buck punched out a little hole in each piece—a hole where an eye would be—and another hole so the piece could be hung up. He fastened a length of thin wire to each finished bit of work.

"They'd look mighty pretty, a-hangin' on somebody's Christmas tree," Ma said.

Ruth Carroll

61

One afternoon Pa was late getting home in the truck. He came fast, and he stopped short. He blew the horn seven times.

The other Tatums came running—Beanie from the barn, Irby from the pigpen, Buck from the tool shed, Serena from the cow pasture, Ma and Annie Mae from the kitchen.

Pa shouted, "Got news for you-all, got news!" He drew some deep breaths as if he had been running hard. He grinned. He went on, "I got a sight o' money for our tobacco, best price I *ever* got. Saw Mrs. Gudger. She told me our mica pretties and all our other pretties had been a-sellin' like hot cakes. The tourist folks bought every single one. She had a heap o' cash for me. I went and paid off all the money I owed at the general store. Now we don't owe nobody a dollar, not a red cent, we don't."

Ma gave Pa a hug. Pa hugged Ma.

Beanie said loudly, "That ole Sally Gudger, she won't get Sassy Boy!"

His brothers and sisters took the words out of his mouth and made a song. They chanted over and over, "That ole Sally Gudger, she won't get Sassy Boy, won't get Sassy Boy, won't get Sassy Boy."

When they stopped, everybody was laughing.

Pa said, "No, she won't. And just to kind o' celebrate, I bought a heap o' goodies. They're in the truck—come look!"

The other Tatums ran to the truck. The young ones scrambled in.

"Lan's alive!" cried Beanie. "Marshmallows and bananas and jellybeans!"

"All-day suckers!" Annie Mae called out.

"Dates and figs and oranges and grapefruits," said Serena. "Yes, and licorice sticks!"

"Peanuts and soda pop," said Buck.

"Chocolate bars and peppermint sticks and sourballs and gumdrops!" yelled Irby.

"Now you young-uns wait till after supper," Ma said firmly, "afore you pile into all those goodies, you hear?"

The young Tatums carried Pa's gifts into the cabin. Their pockets and their hands were full. Beanie and Annie Mae were hopping and skipping and leaping.

After supper, Beanie rode Sass to the old full-o'-holes tree. Tough Enough's nose was up and sniffing. He was yipping and yowping and yapping and running all around the pony.

Sweetie Pie, the skunk, peeked out at Beanie. Fat Stuff, the raccoon, went *chirr-chirr-chirr* from an upper branch and started to climb down.

Beanie pulled a banana from a pocket. He peeled it and broke it in half. He gave half to Sweetie Pie and held up the other hunk to Fat Stuff.

The raccoon never got it. *Whirr-r-r-r*, there was a quick soft sound of wings cutting the air. *"Hey, hey, hey!"* came a hoarse call. A big bird, diving from above, grabbed the banana hunk out of Beanie's hand.

Beanie gave a happy shout, "Midnight!"

His talking crow flapped up to a bough just above. He sat there, pecking and stuffing himself with a busy beak.

"You thievin' ole varmint," Beanie said lovingly. "Reckon you can see a banana from clear in the next county."

Fat Stuff was chuttering with impatience. Beanie gave him part of another banana. He drew out a bag of marshmallows and handed one to Tough Enough and one to Sassy Boy.

"Fat Stuff and Sweetie Pie and Midnight and Tough Enough and Sass," he said, "now you can eat and eat and eat. You can eat till your eyes bung out."

And Beanie stuffed three marshmallows into his mouth.